The Legend of Bucky the Beaver

Earl Bennett

Print information available on the last page.

ISBN: 978-1-4907-9427-3 (sc)
978-1-4907-9426-6 (e)

Our mission is to efficiently provide the world's finest, most comprehensive book publishing service, enabling every author to experience success. To find out how to publish your book, your way, and have it available worldwide, visit us online at www.trafford.com

Trafford rev. 04/16/2019

www.trafford.com
North America & international
toll-free: 1 888 232 4444 (USA & Canada)
fax: 812 355 4082

Bucky the Beaver

Once upon a time, there lived a village of happy beavers down by the river.
The beavers were busy building a new home.

All the beavers pulled their own weight. Each beaver was to bring limbs for the new home.

And they all did, except for one—Bucky.
Bucky got his name because he was bucktoothed.

Bucky was different. He liked to saw on big trees rather than the little ones like
all the other beavers because the little ones would get stuck in his teeth.

Everyone always teased Bucky,

"Hey, Bucky, are you going to drop that big tree today?"

They all laughed

as they carried their little branches to the homesite.

Bucky just kept on working.

"I'll drop this tree and dam the whole creek. Then they'll see. Besides, I like big trees."

Week after week went by, and Bucky was still working on the mighty oak tree. All the other beavers were still teasing him; they teased him every day.

But Bucky just kept on sawing; he liked the big trees.

As summer was drawing to an end, the beavers were working overtime.
They knew that soon the rains would come, and the river would rise.
And with the new home still not completed,

the rains could wash away all that had been done. Then they would have no home for the winter, and that was not a good thing.

It was a cool sunny day as the beavers all worked hard to finish their home.
All day long, as they worked, a big dark cloud moved slowly toward them.
They all knew they were in trouble.

Their new home still needed a roof, and the rains had just started.

Hours later, the rains were very heavy. All the beavers were tired. And with the river water rising each hour, the job of putting on the roof looked impossible.

In spite of the heavy rain, all the beavers kept on working, and Bucky kept on working on his big tree too.

Bucky knew that if he could drop the mighty oak tree, he could save their home.

The water was too deep and swift to work any more. The beavers had to give up the battle against the raging water. It was just too dangerous to continue any longer.

They were all so tired they could hardly move.

Tears began to fill their eyes as the thought of being homeless for the winter began to sink in.

Just as all seemed lost, a loud cracking noise broke the air.

"TIMBER"

CRACK

"Timber!" cried Bucky.
"Timber!"

No one could believe their eyes. The mighty oak was falling right over their new home.

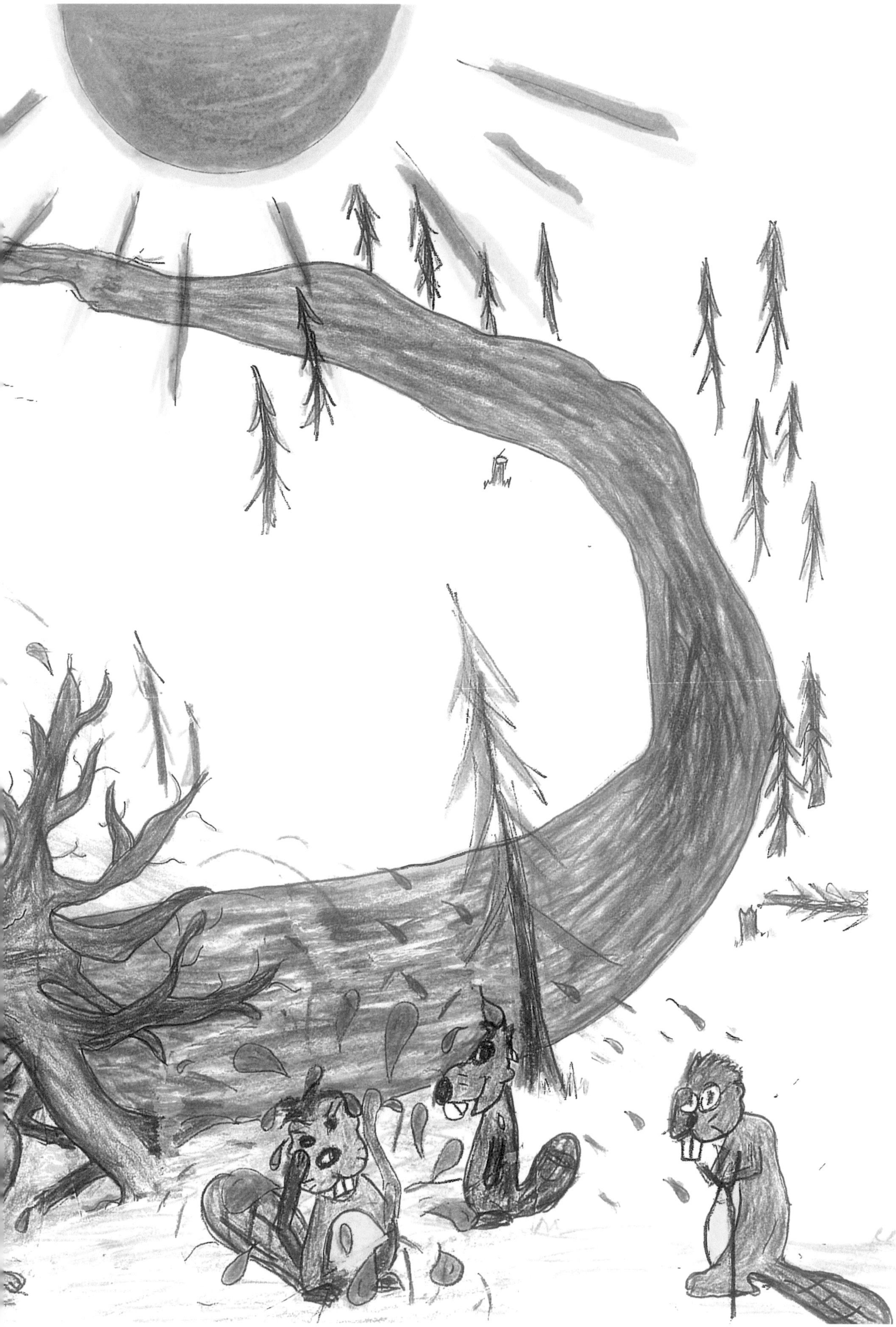

When the water had settled down, they could see that the mighty oak had fallen right over their new home.

It made the perfect roof for their new home, and just in time. The river water was the highest anyone had ever seen. Everyone shouted for joy.

Bucky had saved their home by sticking to it and not giving up even when all the other beavers teased him.

Bucky was a hero.

The heavy rains come and go, but the beaver village and the mighty oak are still there. And so is the legend of the little beaver with an overbite who liked to saw on big trees.

Printed in the United States
By Bookmasters